C000299844

Love
makes the world stand still

This book is dedicated to those, suitable and unsuitable, who have made me go weak at the knees over the years.

First published in the United Kingdom in 2017 by
Portico
1 Gower Street
London
WC1E 6HD

An imprint of Pavilion Books Company Ltd

ISBN 978-1-91104-210-5

A CIP catalogue record for this book is available from the British Library.

10 9 8 7 6 5 4 3 2 1

Design: Suzanne Perkins/grafica
Reproduction by Mission Productions Ltd, Hong Kong
Printed and bound by Toppan Leefung Printing Ltd, China

This book can be ordered direct from the publisher at www.pavilionbooks.com

THE WIT AND
Cath Tate
WISDOM OF

Love

makes the world stand still

PORTICO

Love makes the world
stand still.

Love doesn't make
the world go round.

Love makes the
ride worthwhile.

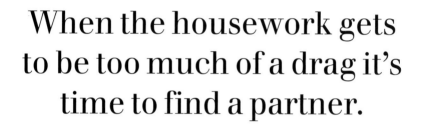

When the housework gets to be too much of a drag it's time to find a partner.

We need more love and less paperwork.

All I want is a stable relationship.

Thanks to the internet, you can always find the perfect partner.

"Finding the perfect pair of shoes is even harder than finding a man."

"I've just found a *beautiful* young man on Grindr."

"I found him on eBay."

She wondered if she was a little overdressed for a first date.

At the beginning,
it pays to show an
interest.

"What does he mean?
'He really likes me but he
needs more space'…"

"Fortunately she is deeply in love with us."

Nothing beats a good holiday romance.

Nobody's perfect,
until you fall in love
with them.

Love is a mixture of desire
and misunderstanding.

The basis of many relationships is unbridled passion.

"You're on my To Do List."

The people you find most attractive are also usually the most unsuitable.

Too much of a
good thing can
be wonderful.

"Come on baby,
light my fire."

"Would you do me the honour of pairing my socks on a permanent basis?"

"I love you enough to irritate all my Facebook friends about it."

"It's high time I made an honest man of you!"

Everyone has their own idea of The Perfect Partner.

"There's no one I'd rather sit next to when I'm checking my phone."

"You're my true soul mate. You know how to load the dishwasher."

At some point you will
have to face
The New Boyfriend
Inspection Team.

Don't worry, if you keep him long enough he'll come back into fashion.

You never forget your first love or your first car.

There is a simple
recipe for a successful
relationship which is
buried somewhere
in the mess on the
kitchen table.

"We have a strange and wonderful relationship.

You're strange and I'm wonderful."

You aren't a true couple until you understand every word the other person hasn't said.

Every relationship is totally bonkers in its own unique way.

It's so great to find that one person you want to annoy for the rest of your life.

When the situation becomes serious a sense of humour becomes vital.

All marriages are happy.
It's living together
afterwards when the
fun begins.

Love conquers all,
except poverty and
toothache.

You only know
what happiness is once
you're married, and
by then it's too late.

If you think women are
the weaker sex, try pulling
the duvet back over to
your side.

"In our house I'm the boss. My wife is just the decision-maker."

Never laugh at your partner's choices. You're one of them.

A good husband listens
even when his wife
is silent.

A good wife listens
even when her husband
is talking.

Behind every talented
woman stands a man
wondering what's for
dinner.

Happy couples enjoy the same pastimes.

FOR SALE

Part-worn husband.
One careful owner.
Will do some
domestic jobs.
Wardrobe in need of
renovation.

Pillars of the community
and addicted to
The Archers.

However much you love someone, there are times when you would love a separate bathroom more.

Familiarity breeds
contempt and children.

"I don't know how you put
up with me.
Then I remembered I put
up with you."

Like a good wine,
a relationship matures
with age.

"It's pretty cool we've been together for however long it is we've been together."

Sometimes it just takes time to admit that you've made the right choice.

It's not *what* you have
in your life but *who*
you have in your life.

Cath Tate has lived and worked in London for more years than she cares to mention. She currently runs a greetings card company, Cath Tate Cards, with her daughter Rosie: the bulk of the photos and captions in this book started life as greetings cards.

The photos have been collected over the years by Cath and her friends in junk shops and vintage fairs. They are all genuine and show people in all their glory, on the beach, on a day out, posing stiffly for the photographer, drinking with friends, smiling or scowling at the camera.

The photographs were all taken sometime between 1880 and 1960. Times change but people, their friendships, their little joys and stupid mistakes, remain the same. Some things have changed though, and Cath Tate has used modern technical wizardry to tease some colour into the cheeks of those whose cheeks lost their colour some time ago.

The quotes that go with the photos come from random corners of life and usually reflect some current concern that is bugging her.

If you want to see all the current greetings cards and other ephemera available from Cath Tate Cards see www.cathtatecards.com

Cath Tate

Many thanks to all those helped me put this book together, including Discordia, who have fed me with wonderful photos and ideas over the years, and Suzanne Perkins, who has made sure everything looks OK, and also has a good line in jokes.

Pictures credits

Photos from the collection of Cath Tate apart from the following:

Discordia/Simon: Pages 8–11, 14–17, 36–37, 62–63, 68–69, 80–81, 88–91, 106–107, 110–111

Keith Allen: 40–41